D0478398

Bea's Bees

Katherine Pryor
Illustrated by Ellie Peterson

For Gaizka & Lia—

Thanks for making our world a better place to be a bee!

Schiffer Publishing Ltd

4880 Lower Valley Road · Atglen, PA 19310

Copyright © 2019 by Katherine Pryor
Illustration copyright © 2019 by Ellie Peterson

Library of Congress Control Number: 2018956667

All rights reserved. No part of this work may be reproduced
or used in any form or by any means—graphic, electronic, or
mechanical, including photocopying or information storage and
retrieval systems—without written permission from the publisher.

The scanning, uploading, and distribution of this book or any part
thereof via the Internet or any other means without the permission
of the publisher is illegal and punishable by law. Please purchase
only authorized editions and do not participate in or encourage
the electronic piracy of copyrighted materials.

"Schiffer," "Schiffer Publishing, Ltd.," and the pen and inkwell logo
are registered trademarks of Schiffer Publishing, Ltd.

Edited by Kim Grandizio
Designed by Brenda McCallum

Type set in Coop Forged/Aaux

ISBN: 978-0-7643-5699-5
Printed in China
Published by Schiffer Publishing, Ltd.
4880 Lower Valley Road
Atglen, PA 19310
Phone: (610) 593-1777; Fax: (610) 593-2002
E-mail: Info@schifferbooks.com
Web: www.schifferbooks.com

For our complete selection of fine books on this and related
subjects, please visit our website at www.schifferbooks.com. You
may also write for a free catalog.

Schiffer Publishing's titles are available at special discounts for
bulk purchases for sales promotions or premiums. Special editions,
including personalized covers, corporate imprints, and excerpts,
can be created in large quantities for special needs. For more
information, contact the publisher.

We are always looking for people to write books on new and
related subjects. If you have an idea for a book, please contact
us at proposals@schifferbooks.com.

For Carson & Bay,
making my world a better place every day.
-kp

For Jordan, who always believes in me.
-ep

Beatrix heard a humming
as she walked through the park on her
way home from school.

She followed the sound to a hollow oak tree.
A cloud of wild bumblebees flew
in and out of a hidden beehive like it was
the world's busiest airport.

Bea crept closer.
The bees flew zig-zags and crazy-eights.
They hovered and dove.
They zipped out fast but flew home slowly,
their tiny bodies weighed down
with pollen and nectar.

Bea visited the hive every day.
She watched the bees flit from flower
to flower, buzzing with happiness
as they collected food for their families.

Then one day, the tree was silent.
A lonely butterfly circled the oak tree,
looking for its friends.

Its friends were gone.

The next day at school,
Bea told her teacher what
happened.

"Where did my bees go?"
She asked.

"I don't know,"
her teacher sighed.
"Sometimes bees just
disappear."

Bea didn't like that one bit.
How could a whole hive disappear?

The park was quiet as she walked home.
Bea looked toward the oak tree,
but even the butterfly was gone.

Then Bea noticed something else—
the flowers around the oak tree
had been cut down.

Beatrix knew that bees like flowers.
It is how they get all of their food.

The next time Bea's class went to the library,
Bea rushed for the librarian.

"What type of flowers do bees like?"

"I don't know,"
the librarian said. "Let's find out."

Bea read everything she could about bees.

She learned that they liked to eat
pollen and nectar from lots of different flowers, and that
they needed lots of open space to find them.

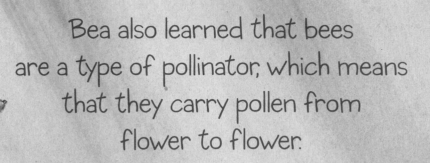

Bea also learned that bees
are a type of pollinator, which means
that they carry pollen from
flower to flower.

Without bees, blueberry, raspberry, and pumpkin plants would not be able to turn their flowers into fruit.

There would be no more apples or almonds or avocados.
Without bees, some of Beatrix's favorite foods would disappear.

Bea began to make a plan.

In the early wet days of spring,
Bea planted wildflower seeds around
the base of her tree. She planted mint and
clover and sunflowers.

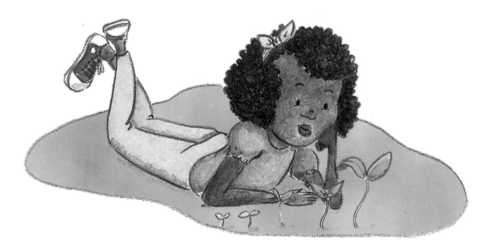

The seedlings began to sprout.

The flowers began to bloom.

But the tree stayed silent.

Bea did her science fair project on bees.

She handed out wildflower seeds
to everyone at school and asked them to
help feed the bees.

All over the neighborhood, their seedlings sprouted.

Their flowers bloomed.

Still, the tree was silent.

Beatrix began to lose hope.
She sat by her tree and cried sad tears at
the thought of losing her bees forever.

Then she heard it.

A single bumblebee buzzed past, landing on one of the sunflowers.

She saw another, and another.
Bees flew out of a nest in the ground
near the hollow oak tree.

They hovered and dove.
They flew zig-zags and crazy-eights.
They zipped out to find pollen and nectar,
then flew home, slow and fat,
to feed their family.

Bea's bees were back.

Be a Friend to Bees

Our world would be very different without bees.

There are about 20,000 species of bees. A small number of those bees make honey, but all bees help people and plants in important ways. As bees buzz from flower to flower in search of nectar and pollen, their legs and bodies collect pollen dust, carrying pollen to every other flower they visit. Some of the pollen rubs off on the flowers' stigmas. When this happens, fertilization can take place, and a fruit can develop. A single bee can visit up to 5,000 flowers in one day!

Many of the foods we love need bees to turn their flowers into fruit. Bees help grow nuts like almonds and cashews, as well as fruits like berries, apples, cherries, kiwis, mangos, pears, peaches, and melons. Pumpkins, tomatoes, and even chocolate all need bees.

Unfortunately, bees are in danger. Some species of bees have been added to the Endangered Species List, meaning that their numbers are becoming so low that they might disappear. There are several reasons for this: the loss of open spaces for bees to find flowers, climate change, and the use of some chemical pesticides that can kill or confuse bees.

The good news? You can help! Plant pollinator gardens at home or school. Ask your parents to buy food raised without chemical pesticides, or grow some of your favorite foods yourself. Write a letter or email to your city council asking them to ban neonicotinoids, a type of pesticide that hurts bees.

Bees help us every day. We—like Bea—can make our world a better place to be a bee.

TRIFOLIUM

BLACK-EYED SUSAN

LAVENDER

ASTER

BORAGE

BEE BALM

ALYSSUM

CONEFLOWER

SNOWDROP

CRANESBILL

CROCUS

HYACINTH

THISTLE

SALVIA

SUNFLOWER

GOLDENROD

SEDUM

COSMOS

What's growing in Bea's garden?